Oh, No, Hippo!

Early ★ Reader

First American edition published in 2022 by Lerner Publishing Group, Inc.

An original concept by Heather Pindar
Copyright © 2022 Heather Pindar

Illustrated by Angelika Scudamore

First published by Maverick Arts Publishing Limited

Maverick
arts publishing

Licensed Edition
Oh, No, Hippo!

Lerner Publications Company
An imprint of Lerner Publishing Group, Inc.
241 First Avenue North
Minneapolis, MN 55401 USA

For reading levels and more information, look up this title at
www.lernerbooks.com.

Main body text set in Mikado a. Typeface provided by HVD Fonts.

Library of Congress Cataloging-in-Publication Data

Names: Pindar, Heather, author. | Scudamore, Angelika, illustrator.
Title: Oh, no, Hippo! / Heather Pindar ; illustrated by Angelika Scudamore.
Description: First American edition. | Minneapolis : Lerner Publications, 2022. | Series: Early bird readers. Blue (Early bird stories) | "First published by Maverick Arts Publishing Limited"—Page facing title page. | Audience: Ages 4–8. | Audience: Grades K–1. | Summary: "Hippo wants to join the other animals in activities, but he is very clumsy. With full-color illustrations and leveled text"— Provided by publisher.
Identifiers: LCCN 2021043310 (print) | LCCN 2021043311 (ebook) | ISBN 9781728438429 (lib. bdg.) | ISBN 9781728448305 (pbk.) | ISBN 9781728444543 (eb pdf)
Subjects: LCSH: Readers (Primary) | LCGFT: Readers (Publications)
Classification: LCC PE1119.2 .P566 2022 (print) | LCC PE1119.2 (ebook) | DDC 428.6/2—dc23

LC record available at https://lccn.loc.gov/2021043310
LC ebook record available at https://lccn.loc.gov/2021043311

Manufactured in the United States of America
1-49665-49585-9/7/2021

Oh, No, Hippo!

Heather Pindar

Illustrated by
Angelika Scudamore

Lerner Publications ◆ Minneapolis

"It's my birthday," said Chimp.

"Let's swing from tree to tree."

Chimp swung.

Flamingo and Zebra swung too.

But not . . .

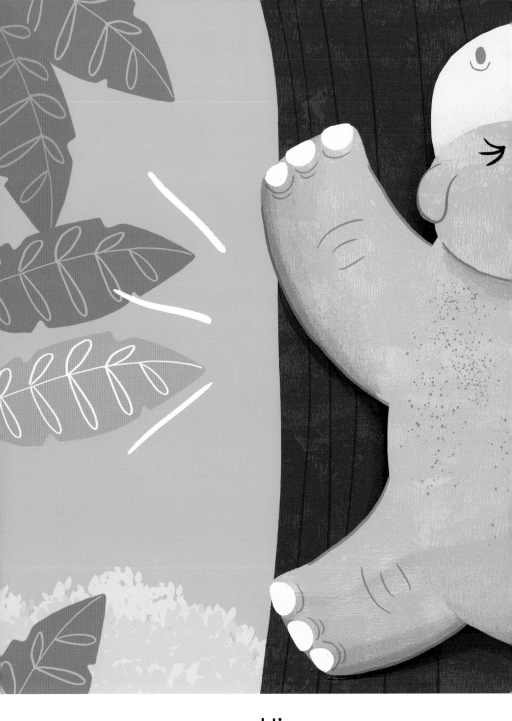

. . . Hippo.

SWISH! BANG! He hit the tree.

SPLAT! Hippo fell into Chimp's birthday cake.

"Oh, no, Hippo!" said everyone.

"It's my birthday," said Zebra.

"Let's run as fast as we can."

Chimp and Flamingo ran after

Zebra. But not . . .

TRIP! THUMP!

Hippo fell into Zebra's birthday cake.

"Oh, no, Hippo!" said everyone.

"It's my birthday," said Flamingo.

"Everyone hop like me."

Hop, hop, hop went Flamingo,
Chimp, and Zebra.

But not . . .

. . . Hippo.

SPIN! CRASH!

SPLAT!

Hippo fell into Flamingo's birthday cake.

"Oh, no, Hippo!" said everyone.

One hot afternoon, Hippo said,

"Let's go for a swim."

Hippo swam.

But not Chimp, Zebra, and Flamingo.

"Hop on my back," said Hippo.

"What fun!" said Zebra.

"This is the best!" said Flamingo.

"I see cakes," said Chimp.

"One . . . two . . . three . . . cakes!"

"Do you like the cakes?" said Hippo.

"Oh YES!" said everyone.

"Thank you, Hippo!"

Quiz

1. What did Monkey do for his birthday?
   a) Run
   b) Swing
   c) Hop

2. What happened to the cakes?
   a) Hippo fell into them
   b) The animals ate them
   c) They were stolen

3. What did Hippo trip on?
   a) A branch
   b) A rock
   c) A tree

4. Who likes swimming?
   a) Flamingo
   b) Zebra
   c) Hippo

5. What did Hippo give at the end?
   a) Party bags
   b) Balloons
   c) New cakes

EARLY BIRD STORIES

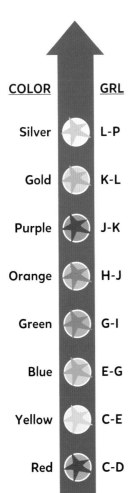

COLOR		GRL
Silver		L-P
Gold		K-L
Purple		J-K
Orange		H-J
Green		G-I
Blue		E-G
Yellow		C-E
Red		C-D
Pink		A-C

Leveled for Guided Reading

Early Bird Stories have been edited and leveled by leading educational consultants to correspond with guided reading levels. The levels are assigned by taking into account the content, language style, layout, and phonics used in each book. Visit www.lernerbooks.com for more Early Bird Readers titles!